To the Grownups who are reading this:

I, You, We: Sparking the Light in Me helps children connect with themselves and the world around them. Through reading and exploring the exercises in this book with your child, you can spark rich conversations about ways to build loving relationships, empathy for others, and confidence in your child's self-worth.

We hope this book will ignite your child's curiosity and show them that we are all very much the same, and unique in our own special way. By expressing ourselves fully, we have the power to create anything we want in life!

Sincerely,
Atlas SF14 Team

Second paperback edition April 2022

Illustrations by Fernando Labarca Hurtado

ISBN 979-8-4160-1949-5

Independently published by the Atlas SF14 Team.
www.SparkTheLightInMe.com

You start as a precious baby,
and everything is about "Me!"

As we grow,
our curiosity grows,
and we ask questions
about the world around us.

What are some questions you
would like to ask about the world?

Asking questions to the important people in your life helps us feel closer to them.

What was their favorite thing to do when they were your age?

You are not just a "Me."

You have people who care
about you – you are a "We!"

Listening is one of the ways we show people we care and love them.

How can you show you are listening carefully?

When we share stories with someone, we are connecting with them in a special way.

Asking questions and listening brings us closer.

Who do you enjoy sharing stories with?

Trust is the feeling we
can count on someone.

People we trust protect us,
tell us the truth, and
care about how we are.

If you are honest and caring,
people will trust you.

Who do you trust?

Being trustworthy also means doing what we say we will do.

What things do you do to help out, and do you do them when you say you will?

When you feel angry,
stop and take a breath.
Count to ten. Then tell
someone how you feel.

Talking about our feelings
helps us feel better.

Who can you talk to
about your feelings?

Empathy is the ability to understand someone else's feelings.

We often do not know how someone feels inside.

Reaching out and showing we care can help us feel like we are not alone.

Who can you reach out to?

Forgiveness means accepting an apology from someone who hurt us.

If we believe they are honest, we can let go of our hurt and feel better.

Who can you forgive?

We are all born
as precious babies.

Everyone is a little different,
but we all share many of
the same things inside.

In what ways are your
friends the same as you?

You are a special
and unique person.

There is no one else
exactly like you.

What you do matters.

What can you do to make a
difference in the world?

Be kind and give to others. If you
show kindness to someone
every day, what might happen?

Every day we have the chance to bring happiness into someone's life. How can you spark happiness in someone else?

A tree is a living being, just like
a flower, a bird, and you!

Seeing and being with plants and
animals helps us feel joy and
connection to our earth.

What do you enjoy seeing,
touching, or hearing when
you are outside?

We all live together on
the same planet.

How can we take care of it and
keep it clean for all of us?

When we listen, share, and use our voice, we can make a powerful difference within our families and our community.

When we connect to and care for nature, we can heal our beautiful earth.

What is something you can do today to make a difference in our world?

Dear Grownups:

Thank you for reading I, You, We: Sparking the Light in Me. Here are a few suggestions for activities and questions to bring the topics in the book to life.

1) Discover the "I" by having both of you draw a self-portrait and describing what you drew.

2) Create an act of kindness. Talk about what you did and how being kind made you feel.

3) Look around your neighborhood. What is one action you can take to help the planet? Talk about why this is important.

Discussion Questions:

1) How can you be kind without using words?

2) If you could have any animal as your friend,
   which animal would you pick and why?

3) Think about a time when you felt sad. Why
   did you feel sad? What helped you feel better?

4) Imagine you are playing outside.
   What are you doing? How do you feel?

About The Atlas Project

Atlas is a nonprofit organization that believes if we all lived lives focused on vision, responsibility, integrity, service, and presence, we can create communities that are better for everyone.

Atlas empowers you to create extraordinary results in the areas of your life that matter to you the most.

www.AtlasProject.org